S0-EHY-404

bertha
and the Windmills
Story by **Eric Charles**
Pictures by **Steve Augarde**
from the original television designs by **Ivor Wood**
From the BBC TV Series

ANDRE DEUTSCH

First published in 1985 by
André Deutsch Limited
105 Great Russell Street London WC1B 3LJ

Text copyright © 1985 by Eric Charles
Illustrations copyright © 1985 by André Deutsch Limited
and Woodland Animations Limited
All rights reserved

British Library Cataloguing in Publication Data

Charles, Eric
  Bertha and the windmills.
  I. Title   II. Augarde, Steve   III. Wood, Ivor
  823′.914[J]   PZ7

  ISBN 0–233–97814–3

It was lunchtime at Spottiswood and Company and Bertha, the big machine, had stopped work.

She had been making windmill money-boxes, specially designed by
Mr Sprott to make saving money a pleasure.

Ted had gone to the canteen for his lunch, while Roy and Nell were sitting

on a packing case eating their sandwiches and watching TOM the robot cleaning Bertha.

"Peep—Peep," sounded TOM as he polished the cogs and wheels.

"It's jolly useful having a robot that doesn't need to stop for lunch," said Roy. He took a bite, making a loud crunching noise. Nell looked at him.

"What's in that sandwich?" she asked.

"Peanut butter and cornflakes." He opened the sandwich to show her.

"Peanut butter and CORNFLAKES!" said Nell in amazement.

"Very nice," said Roy, "Would you like to try one?"

"No thank you," said Nell, "I prefer my own."

"What are they?" asked Roy.

"Cheese and cucumber."

"Sounds tasty." Roy looked around. "Where's Flo?" he asked.

"Gone shopping," said Nell. "She'll be hungry when she comes back, so I'll save her one of my sandwiches." She wrapped up a sandwich and put it on one side.

Roy pointed to one of the windmills Bertha had made. "Jolly good idea of Mr Sprott's that, making a windmill into a money-box," he said.

"When you put your money in the top," said Nell, "the sails go round and it plays a tune."

"Does it?" Roy went to the packing table. "I'd like to try that," he said. He rummaged in his overall pockets, found some coins and put one in the slot. The sails began to turn and there was a tinkling sound of music.

"That's a pretty tune," said Nell.

They listened until the music stopped. "I like that," said Roy, and put another coin in the slot.

TOM stopped polishing and came to listen. He liked the tinkling sound of the music. "Peep—Peep," he said.

Roy laughed. "TOM wants to play it," he said. He found a coin and gave it to TOM. The clever little robot took it and carefully placed it in the windmill. When the sails turned and the music played, TOM 'peeped' with delight.

"Does it play any other tunes?" asked Roy.

"I don't know," said Nell. "Let's find out." She opened her purse and took out a coin. "This is all I've got," she said and put it in the slot.

"It's the same tune," said Roy. "Do you think people will get tired of it?"

"Of course not," said Nell. "They won't be putting money in all the time, will they?"

"No, I suppose not." Roy picked the windmill up and shook it. He turned it round and looked at the back. "How do you get the money out?" he asked. "There's no key."

"I don't remember Bertha making any keys," said Nell.

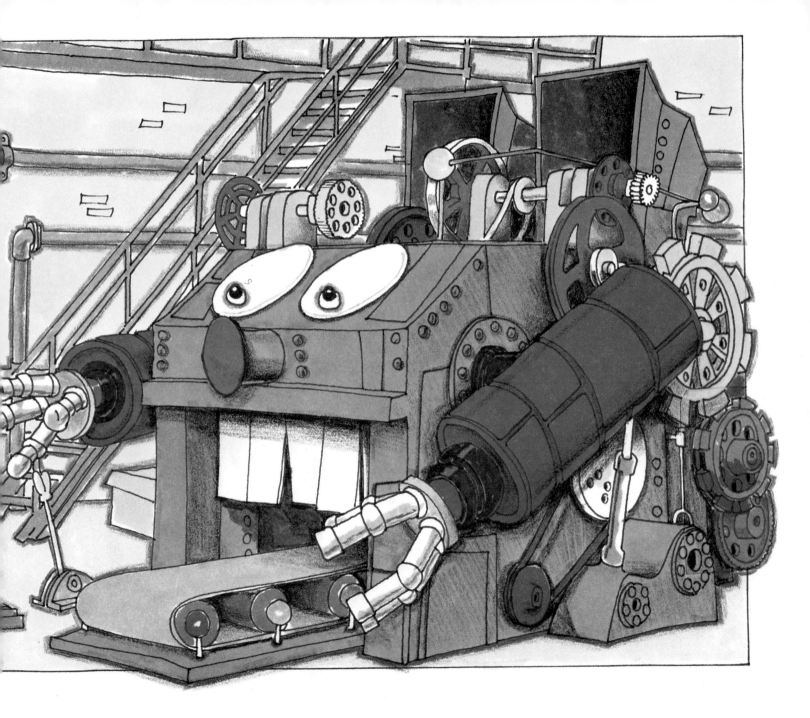

When Ted came back from the canteen, Roy told him about the windmill money-box. Ted put a coin in the windmill and it worked beautifully. "The shops will sell a lot of these," he said.

"Not without a key," said Nell. "What's the good of saving money if you can't get it out?"

Ted looked at the papers on his clipboard.

"It doesn't say anything here about Bertha having to make keys," he said.

Mr Duncan, the factory foreman, came to see what all the chatter was about. "Come on, come on," he said, "Why hasn't Bertha started work?"

"We're having trouble with these money-boxes," Ted told him.

The foreman looked at the windmill. "Looks all right to me," he said.

"Put a coin in the slot and see what happens," said Roy.

The sails of the windmill spun around and the music played.

"Nothing wrong with that," said Mr Duncan.

"Try getting your money out," said Roy.

Mr Duncan opened his purse and, reluctantly, took out the smallest coin he could find. "I'm not sure I can spare this," he said and dropped it into the slot.

"What do you mean?" The foreman picked up the money-box and examined it. He shook it; he peered into the slot and tried to poke his finger in.

He turned it upside down and thumped the bottom. No coins came out.

"You can't open it because there's no key," Roy told him.

"No key, eh? And whose fault is that?" demanded the foreman.

He pointed at Bertha. "Has that machine been playing up again?"

A low rumbling came from inside Bertha. Ted patted her. "It's not Bertha's fault," he said. "She's the best machine in the factory. There was no design for making a key."

Bertha stopped rumbling and Ted patted her again. "It's all right," he said, quietly.

The foreman took the windmill. "I'll show this to Mr Willmake," he said.

"Well, I suppose we'd better start work," said Ted. Then he looked around. "Where's Flo?"

"She's gone shopping," said Nell.

Ted looked at his watch. "She's late," he said.

In the office, Mr Willmake, the manager, was looking at the windmill. Both he and his secretary, had put money in the slot and watched it working. Miss McClackerty liked the tinkling tune so much she played it twice.

"The only trouble is, sir, you can't get the money out," said Mr Duncan. He picked the windmill up and rattled it. "There's one of MY coins in there, too."

"It sounds as if there are a lot of coins in there," said Mr Willmake. "We'd better ask Mr Sprott, it's one of his specials. Ask Mr Sprott to come and see me, please, Miss McClackerty."

Downstairs, in the factory, Flo had arrived back at last, looking terribly upset. She sat down on a packing case. "Oh, dear!" she sniffed, "What am I going to do?"

Everyone gathered around her. "What's the matter, Flo?" asked Ted.

"I lost my purse on the way to the shops." Flo blew into her handkerchief. "I've been looking for it everywhere. That's why I'm late back. I'm sorry Ted."

Nell put her arm around her. "Poor old Flo," she said.

Flo sniffed again. "Oh, I'm so careless," she said. "All my money gone."

"Look, I've saved you something to eat," said Nell, trying to cheer her up. She gave her the cheese and cucumber sandwich.

"Thank you," sniffed Flo. "I'd better take it home for my supper, I couldn't buy any food." She left the sandwich wrapped and put it in her coat pocket.

"Maybe you dropped your purse here," said Ted. "Let's have a good look for it."

"Righto," said Roy.

"Good idea," said Nell.

"Peep—Peep," said TOM, and they all started to look for Flo's purse.

Upstairs, Mr Sprott was in the manager's office. "That windmill money-box is one of my best designs. What's the trouble?" he asked.

"The trouble is," said Mr Willmake. "That we can't get the money out."

"No you can't," replied Mr Sprott, "not until it is full.

"It's specially designed to help people save money. The last coin, the one that fills it, turns the sails the other way. It plays a different tune, the back opens and all the money falls out."

"Ah, that's nice," said Miss McClackerty.

Mr Willmake chuckled. "Very clever, Mr Sprott."

Mr Duncan said, "I'll take it downstairs and show Ted how it works. He thought it ought to have a key." He picked up the windmill and went out, followed by Mr Sprott and the manager.

Downstairs in the factory, Panjid drove up in his forklift truck and pointed to the boxes of windmills. "Are those for the dispatch department?" he asked Ted. Ted shook his head. "Not yet, Panjid. We don't know how they work."

"We do know how they work!" called Mr Willmake coming down the stairs. "Mr Sprott will show you."

Mr Sprott took the windmill and placed it on the packing table.

"This money-box is almost full," he said. "It needs just one more coin for you to see how it works." He held out in his hand. "Coin, please, anyone?"

Nell searched her purse and shook her head. "I've put all mine in already," she said.

"So have I," said Roy.

"I've no money," said Ted.

"Peep–Peep," said TOM.

"I have a coin," said Panjid, offering it to Mr Sprott.

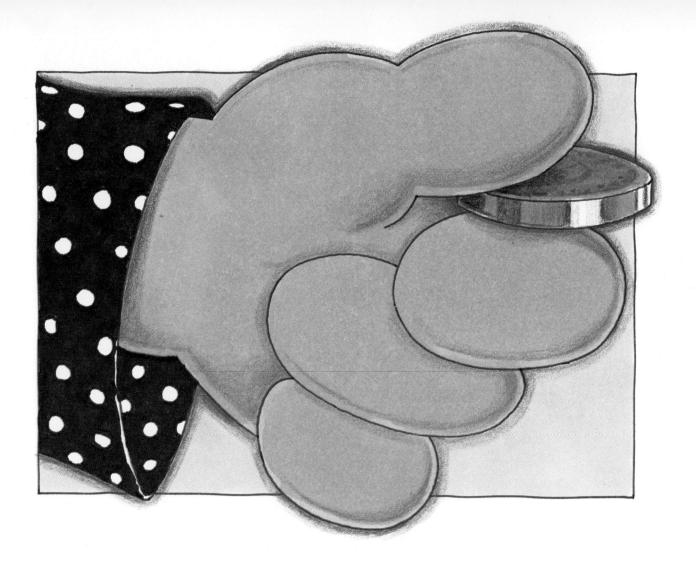

"Just pop it in there." Mr Sprott pointed to the slot in the top of the windmill.

Panjid put the coin in the slot.

The sails on the windmill turned the other way and it played a different tune.
When the music stopped, the back opened and all the coins came jingling out.

"BINGO!" cried Panjid. "Have I won the JACKPOT?"
"Sorry, Panjid, that money belongs to all of us," said the manager.

"Look, Mr Willmake, if everyone agrees, I think we should give the money to Flo," said Ted. "You see, she's lost her purse."

"Of course Flo must have the money. What a splendid idea, Ted." Everyone agreed.

"Thank you all very much." Flo collected the coins, happy to have such good workmates.

"That's a very clever money-box, Mr Sprott," said Nell. "I'm sure lots of people will buy them, but how will they know how they work?"

"The instructions are printed on the box," said Mr Sprott.

Nell picked up a box and looked at it. On the top was a picture of the windmill and on the bottom, printed very clearly, were the instructions. "Well, I never!" exclaimed Nell. "So they are. I never thought to look."

Mr Sprott wagged his finger at her. "Remember, Nell, always read the instructions on the box."

"All right everyone, back to work," called Ted. He switched Bertha on and listened. She sounded happy. "Good old Bertha," he said.